Hello, Star

For Henry.
If it wasn't for your tender six-year-old heart,
this book wouldn't exist.
— SVWL

For my mom.
— VH

PUFFIN BOOKS

UK | USA | Canada | Ireland | Australia
India | New Zealand | South Africa

Puffin Books is part of the Penguin Random House group of companies
whose addresses can be found at global.penguinrandomhouse.com.

www.penguin.co.uk   www.puffin.co.uk   www.ladybird.co.uk

First published in the USA by Little, Brown and Company 2021
Published in Great Britain by Puffin Books 2022

001

Text copyright © Stephanie V.W. Lucianovic, 2021
Illustrations copyright © Vashti Harrison, 2021

The moral right of the author and illustrator has been asserted

Printed in Italy

The authorized representative in the EEA is Penguin Random House Ireland,
Morrison Chambers, 32 Nassau Street, Dublin D02 YH68

A CIP catalogue record for this book is available from the British Library

ISBN: 978–0–241–48894–2

All correspondence to:
Puffin Books, Penguin Random House Children's
One Embassy Gardens, 8 Viaduct Gardens, London, SW11 7BW

Hello, Star

By **Stephanie V.W. Lucianovic**

Illustrated by **Vashti Harrison**

PUFFIN

One winter night, a light shone in the dark sky, brighter than any star, brighter than any planet.

Far, far away, a girl who was young and new and bright and strong was curious about the light.

"It's a supernova," her mother explained. "A very big star is dying. It will shine like that for a long time until it finally fades away."

The girl felt her heart pinch at the idea of the star slowly losing its light all the way out there on its own. She bent her knees and jumped, even though she knew she couldn't reach something so far away.

Before the girl crawled into bed that night, she looked out of her window and whispered, "Hello, Star. I know you're scared, but you're not alone."

At school, the girl usually let others do the talking. But now she had questions of her own. Her teacher pointed to a chart of the solar system and told her that our galaxy, the Milky Way, is thick with stars, and that the closest one to Earth is the sun.

But the girl wanted to know more, so she went to the library and carried home slipping stacks of books to read with her parents.

Night after night, the girl brushed her
teeth, put on her pyjamas, and stood at
her window to say, "Hello, Star. Don't
worry, I know you're out there."

When the girl got older, she could read books to herself. She discovered that stars have different colours, sizes and temperatures, and that her star was a blue supergiant, the largest of all.

She also read that blue supergiants don't usually flare brightly enough to be seen from Earth. That meant her star was special.

The girl became a young woman who studied long into the inky nights, and she began to understand what might happen at the end of her star's life.

It could become a neutron star, made of material so heavy that a teaspoon of its shimmering, blazing star stuff would weigh as much as a mountain. Her star could become a black hole, pulling in light and mysteries at the same time.

She longed to solve those mysteries. And she realized that reading, and studying, and watching from afar weren't enough for her. "Hello, Star," she whispered. "I'll find a way to you."

She practised flying

and ate while floating in mid-air.

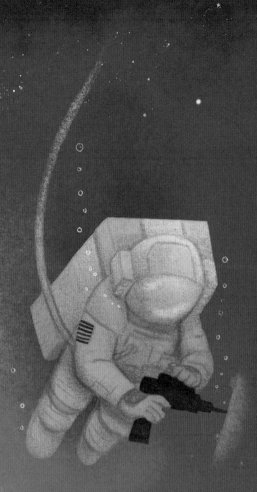

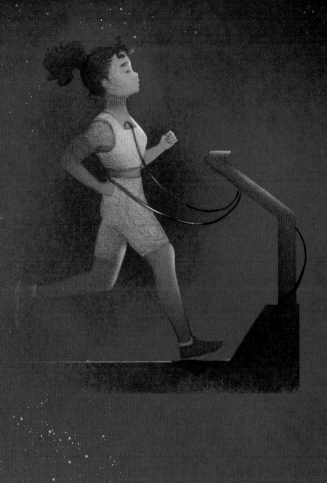

She fixed machines

and ran for miles.

When the woman felt frustrated and tired, she looked up at her patient star, waiting so far out in space, and took a deep breath. She knew from her careful calculations and from telescopes as big as an entire room that her star was getting dimmer.

They were running out of time.

So one night, after working harder than ever, she said,
"Hello, Star. I'm coming."

Now other people listened to the woman, because she knew a great deal about stars and planets and moons and space. She told them about the icy rings of Saturn and about Pluto's frozen heart. She told them about the wild, spinning, red-eyed storm on Jupiter that has lasted hundreds of years.

Every moment brought her closer to the long trip she would take, and the woman felt a spark of excitement and hope in her heart.

At last she stepped aboard a ship.

She zoomed through pale blue skies, zipped past plumped white pillows of clouds, and flew far beyond Earth's atmosphere.

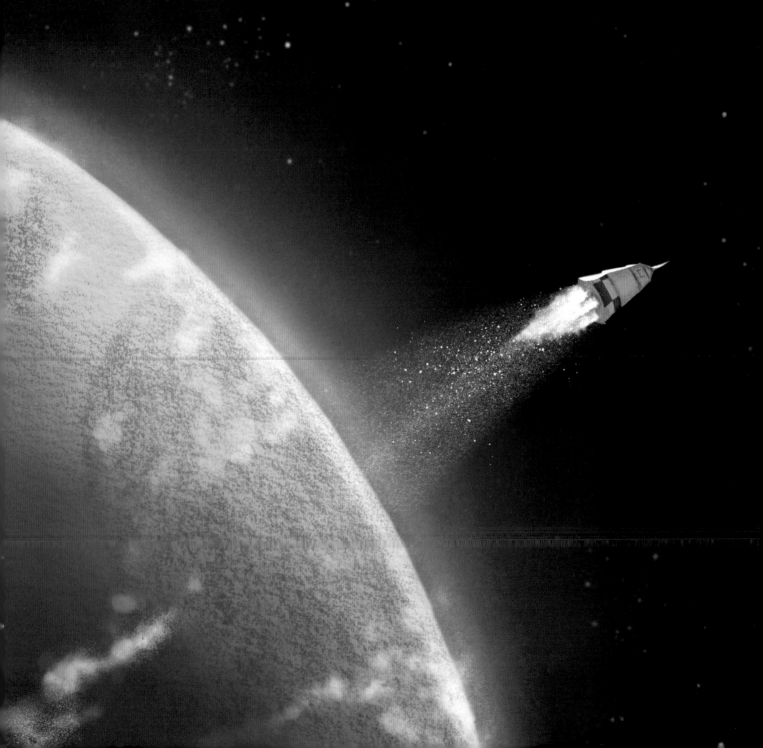

She travelled along an endless velvet night that stretched itself in all directions. And she didn't stop until she was hundreds of thousands of miles away from home.

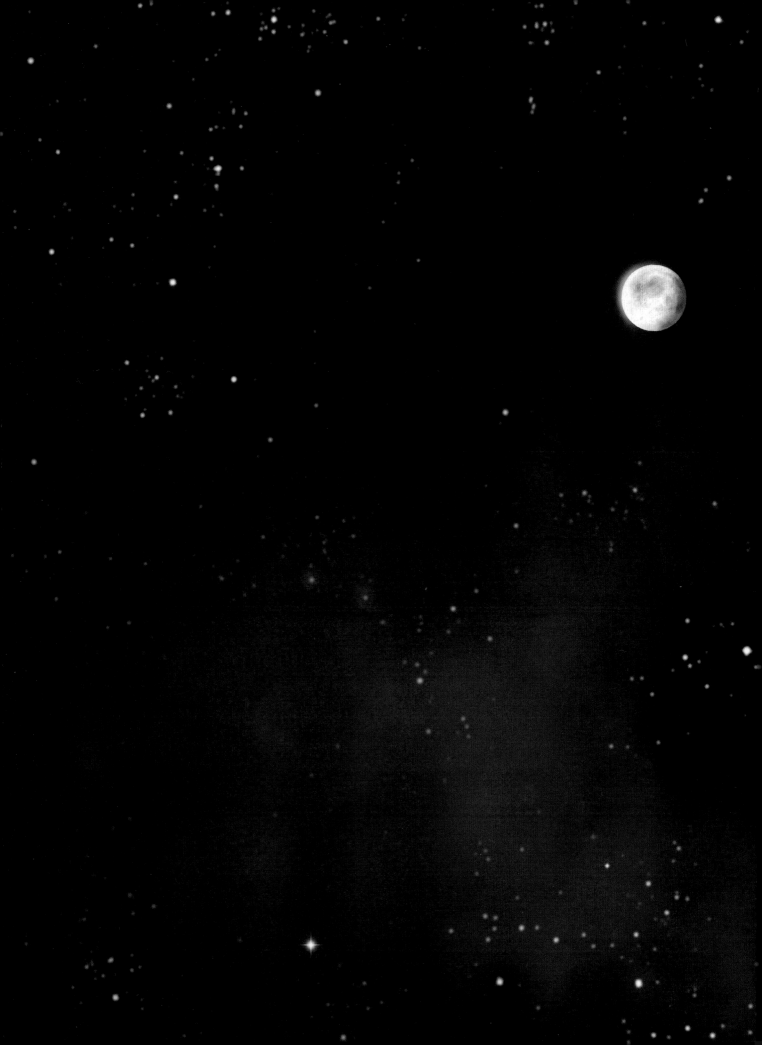

On her first day in space, the woman took a walk by the
light of the Earth.

In the cold, dark silence, surrounded by four hundred
billion stars, she bent her knees and jumped. On the
moon, she could reach higher than ever before.

And the woman, who was still the hopeful girl who
had watched and studied and loved a distant tangle
of light and fire for all these years, stretched out
her hand to her patient friend:

"Hello, Star.
I'm here."

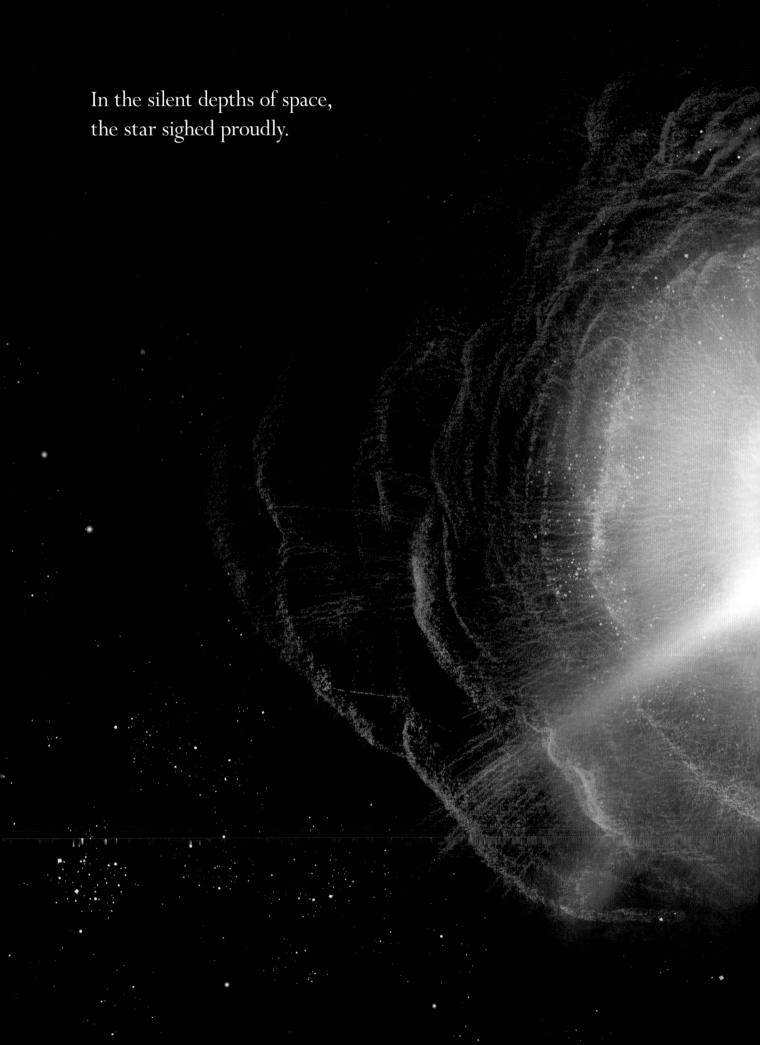

In the silent depths of space,
the star sighed proudly.

And as the tired blue giant finally faded to dark, it cracked into many more stars, all of them young and new and bright and strong.

AUTHOR'S NOTE

Six years ago, my son Henry asked me one day, "Did you know stars die? Isn't that sad?" The striking empathy he had for distant balls of gas turned on a light of inspiration within me. How might a child, full of care and compassion, react upon finding out that stars do not last forever? How might this realization drive his or her life? And out came *Hello, Star*, a fictional story about a girl who loved a star and a star that loved her back.

My second inspiration came from a real supernova of a blue supergiant star in 1987. It was bright enough to be seen on Earth from 168,000 light-years away (that's one *quintillion* – or 1,000,000,000,000,000,000 – miles!). The supernova was called SN 1987A, and it happened in a galaxy known as the Large Magellanic Cloud. Even to this day, scientists are able to observe how the site of that former star continues to evolve and to give birth to more stars and more life. While the girl in this story couldn't really have seen the final moments of her star's life from the surface of the moon, it's amazing to think that a star's life never really ends – it just becomes something new.

Dr Carl Sagan, a famous astronomer, once said: "We are a way for the universe to know itself. Some part of our being knows this is where we came from. We long to return. And we can, because the cosmos is also within us. We're made of star stuff." What he meant was that elements found inside every human body, inside you and me, originally came from a star that exploded a long, long, long time ago. These bits and pieces of stars work together to make you young and new and bright and strong. Every day, ask yourself: "What will I do with my star stuff today?" Then go out and shine.

To learn more about stars and supernovas, visit NASA.gov or head to the nearest library.

—SVWL

NEED
MY
SPACE
when I grow up
ASTRONOMY
COSMOS
ASIMOV
N.K.JEMISIN
BUTLER
HAWKING

TO THE STARS

GOALS
graduate